Thomas Randolph Price

The Construction and Types of Shakespeare's Verse

as seen in the Othello

Thomas Randolph Price

The Construction and Types of Shakespeare's Verse
as seen in the Othello

ISBN/EAN: 9783337391584

Printed in Europe, USA, Canada, Australia, Japan

Cover: Foto ©Andreas Hilbeck / pixelio.de

More available books at **www.hansebooks.com**

Papers of the N. Y. Shakespeare Society.

No. 8.

The Construction and Types

OF

Shakespeare's Verse

AS SEEN IN THE

OTHELLO

By THOMAS R. PRICE, M. A., LL. D.

First Vice-President of the Shakespeare Society of New York.

NEW YORK:

Press of the New York Shakespeare Society.

1888.

INTRODUCTION.

On the 20th of May, 1886, I had the honor of reading a paper on the construction and the types of Shakspere's verse before the Shakspere Society of New York. In that paper I gave the outline and the approximate results that are to be found in this little book ; but in the book I have given to the outline a precision, and to the results an accuracy of statistics that I could not give in the original paper. By confining the examination to the single play of Othello, which I take as a fair example of Shakspere's mature manner, I have sought to give for other work done at other times of the poet's life, a secure basis of study and comparison. The great types of verse, whose existence and ratios I define in the Othello, will be found to exist, indeed, but to exist in varying ratios in all Shakspere's dramatic poems. The study of these variations, so as to reach the law of Shakspere's progress in the construction of verse, seems to me the best way now open to the criticism of Shakspere's style.

For ease of reference, I have followed the text and the numbering of verses that are given in the Globe edition, by Clark and Wright: London, Macmillan & Co., 1884.

THOS. R. PRICE.

COLUMBIA COLLEGE,
    NEW YORK, 15 Jan., 1888.

CONSTRUCTION AND TYPES OF SHAKSPERE'S VERSE

AS SEEN IN THE OTHELLO.

———

The famous saying of Mr. Swinburne, that
'the essential qualities of poetry are imagination and harmony,' is capable of being applied
even to the poetry of Shakspere. In speaking of him, we should indeed have to add a
few hundred other essential qualities to Mr.
Swinburne's two; but after all, even in Shakspere, the qualities that are most permanently
visible are precisely his imagination and his
harmony. Yet in the modern schools of Shaksperian criticism these two essential qualities of
his art have been studied with strangely unequal
attention. The method and the range of his
imagination have been treated by the greatest
critics of modern times in the deepest and most

fruitful way; but the method and the range of his harmony have been either not treated at all, or else treated in ways that led to scant, or to false results. Students of Shakspere have never, indeed, ceased to feel the charm of that vast and infallible harmony which moves in the movement of his words. Great actors of Skakspere, from his day to ours, have never ceased to bring out for each generation, by the penetrating sympathy of their own genius, the rich and intricate cadences of his verses. But the scientific study of his system of verse-construction has been strangely neglected. Even now the student of Shakspere can find little in his text-books to help him toward understanding the principles of his art, or toward the right reading of a vast number of his most memorable verses. For this neglect there can be only two adequate reasons: either the harmonies of Shakspere are so simple as not to need any scientific explanation; or else they are so complex as not to admit of any analysis or solution. No man is likely, I think, to allege that Shakspere's verses are so simple of construction as to make all effort at explanation needless. Nay, even to men of his own time, even to poets that used the same form of verse and spoke words with the same accents as the master himself, there was in Shakspere's verses an element of mysterious effect, of deeply calculated, inscrutable art, that filled them with wonder and awe. Thus Ben Jonson, in his sublime poem of 1623, says of his 'star of poets,' his 'sweet swan of Avon':

> . . . 'the race
> Of Shakspere's mind and manner brightly shines
> In his well-turned and true-filéd lines,
> In each of which he seems to shake a lance
> As brandished at the eyes of ignorance.'

Here Jonson, in this praise of his great rival, praise as honest and wise as it is ardent, shows us two things: first that, in the opinion of the greatest critic of that age, of Jonson himself, the harmony of Shakspere, his construction of 'well-turned and true-filed lines,' was one of the two paramount excellences of his art; and second, that this harmony was attained by means unknown to the vulgar poets of his age, by secrets that eluded, that defied and almost shocked the minds of the ignorant. It is worth while, then, to make a study of Shakspere's manner of verse-construction, in order to see whether we can discover any of the principles by which he worked, or whether in truth the problems of his art must be left as too complex for analysis and explanation.

Among the few that have treated of Shakspere's versification, Dr. Edwin Guest, who treats it as part of English versification and of rhythmical art in general, is by far the greatest. In him I find what seems the key to Shakspere's manner of construction; and when I venture to go beyond what he has expressly taught, I am only developing and expanding what I judge to be implied in his teaching. The work of Dr. Guest, his History of English Rhythms, was published in 1838. It was, however, so far in advance of the English scholarship of those times that it did not much affect the theories nor the schemes of textbook writers. Even now the English and American books that teach versification show

no knowledge of Dr. Guest's system. But in
1869, Dr. J. H. Heinrich Schmidt published
his *Leitfaden in der Rhythmik der Griechen
und Römer.* The German scholar, absolutely
independent of Dr. Guest's system, ignorant,
so far as I know, of even the existence of the
English book, brought to recognition in the
classical poetry the same principles that Dr.
Guest had brought to light in the English. In
1882, the second edition of Guest's History of
English Rhythms, with many useful additions
and corrections, was given to the world by Dr.
Skeat. The book is cumbrous and unwieldy,
badly proportioned and badly arranged; but
the amount of useful matter and of scientific
truth contained in the great volume makes it
a true monument of literature.

In the old systems of metre, such as we used
to study in our childhood, all reduced itself to
a scansion of separate feet. In a mechanical
way, with dire loss of high poetic effect, this
system served to explain to us the movement
of Homer's hexameters and of Vergil's, of the
dialogue of the Greek drama and of Horace's

iambics. It failed, however, to explain to us the movement of the lyrical parts of the drama, and many of the noblest odes of Sophocles and the rest were for us masses of dislocated prose, which each editor had the right, according to his own discretion, to divide into uncouth lines. So in English poetry, that old scansion by feet served well enough to explain to boys the ups and downs of purely mechanical verse. But it failed to explain the movement of the old ballad; it failed to explain the stately march of Milton's blank verse; most of all and worst of all, it failed to interpret the freedom and grace of Shakspere's matchless cadences. These had, indeed, a charm of rhythm that even our ignorance could not hide from us; but, if the system of scansion by feet was true, then the full half, the better half, of Shakspere's verses were incorrect and lawless. The science of prosody had worked, then, to this strange result. The verses of mechanical poets would scan every time, foot by foot, with unfailing precision; hence the school of mechanical versifiers was

correct. But the verses of Shakspere would
not scan ; hence the poetry of Shakspere was
incorrect, and the great poet only 'a gifted
barbarian.'

Now, it was the great achievement of Dr.
Guest to break down, so far as English verse
is concerned, the system of scansion by feet.
Thirty years later, as we have seen, Dr. Schmidt,
from the side of Greek poetry also, laid bare
the falseness of the old scanning. Now, by
the light cast upon English poetry from the
perfect system of Greek verse-forms, we seem
to be at length enabled to rise above the
old misconceptions and to understand the
laws by which the rhythmical genius of Shakspere expressed itself in forms of endless
variety and of never-failing beauty.

If the old system might be described as the
scansion by feet, the new system may be
described as the scansion by staves. This
word, used by Dr. Guest, and taken by him
from the older poetic literature, is in all ways
a good and useful technical term. It is identical in meaning with the *rhythmical series,*

which is the technical term of the modern science of Greek and Roman metres. Let us see, then, what is the stave, or rhythmical series in English poetry.

The stave is a group of feet, from one to four in number, which can be pronounced together, without pause, upon one breath, and be dominated by one accent. As such it is the definite unity of English verse-formation. The English stave can, indeed, if we choose, be analysed into its separate feet, and broken up into trochees and dactyls. But this breaking up of the stave into separate feet is something scholastic and artificial. The stave in its nature is indivisible, living and moving all together, the unit of verse-construction. The poet's mind in the act of composition works not upon the foot, but upon the stave. He builds up his verses, not by adding foot to foot in monotonous succession, but by joining stave to stave in endless variety. Thus, to read Shakspere's verses in the spirit with which he wrote them, we must give up the scansion by feet, which he did not regard, and

follow the scansion by staves, which was for
him the law of rhythmical creation.

From the history of English poetry, which
in this respect is unbroken from Beowulf to
Tennyson, it is possible to find out what staves
exist in our language, and which are best
adapted to our English speech.

In the first place, we have to do with staves
of different lengths. The shortest stave may
have only one accent, the longest may have
four accents. Thus, according to length, there
are four kinds of staves, staves of one accent,
staves of two, staves of three, and staves of
four accents, *e. g.* :

'Devil,' *Othello* IV, 1, 251; 'never,' IV, 2, 8,
is a stave of one accent, a single trochee.

'What's the matter?' IV, 1, 50, a stave of
two accents, a trochaic dipody ($-\cup-\cup$).

'How if fair and foolish?' II, 1, 136, a
stave of three accents, a trochaic tripody
($-\cup-\cup-\cup$).

'You have little cause to say so,' II, 1, 109,
a stave of four accents, a trochaic tetrapody
($-\cup-\cup-\cup-\cup$).

In the second place, according to the way of
ending, the stave may end either with accent
or without accent.   The final trochee, or the
final dactyl, of the stave may be either full or
catalectic,[1] *e. g.*

'What's the matter?' IV, 1, 50, is a stave of
two accents ending full.

'Worse and worse,' II, 1, 135, is a stave of
two accents ending catalectic.

This distinction between the full stave and
the catalectic stave becomes for Shakspere's
art a point of the highest importance.   It
involves the distinction between the masculine and the feminine caesura, and also the
distinction between verses of strong ending
and verses of weak ending.   Shakspere uses
both kinds of caesura and both kinds of ending, and the alternation between the opposed
forms is one of the chief causes of his variety.

So far I have spoken of the staves only in
respect of their length, as staves of one accent,

---

[1] The term *catalectic* is used of rhythmical series in
which the unaccented syllable is cut from the end of
the final foot, so as to give an accented close.

or of two, or of three, or of four, as full or
catalectic. But, before we can fully understand
the variety of English staves, we have to con·
sider not only their length, but also their
inward structure. This depends upon the
nature and the grouping of the feet that make
up each stave. The two kinds of feet that
enter into English staves are trochees and dactyls. The trochee of English poetry consists
of an accented syllable followed by one syllable
out of accent, *e. g. heavy,* ($-\smile$). The dactyl
of English poetry consists of an accented
syllable followed by two syllables out of accent,
e. g. heavily ($-\smile\smile$).[1] Now, all staves that
exist in English poetry are formed either out
of pure trochees, or out of pure dactyls, or
out of dactyls mingled with trochees.

The trochaic stave begins with an accented
syllable and puts one weak syllable after each
strong one, *e. g.* 'Is not this man jealous?'
III, 4, 99 ($-\smile-\smile-\smile$).

---

[1] In using these convenient terms and symbols of the
classical prosody, the accented syllable is regarded as
strong, the unaccented syllable as weak. There is no
reference made to the length of syllables.

The dactylic stave begins with an accented syllable and puts two weak syllables after each strong one, *e. g.* " E'en from the çast to the west,' IV, 2, 144 ($\angle \smile \smile - \smile \smile -$).

The mixed, or logaoedic, stave begins with an accented syllable, and varies the number of weak syllables, according to a definite plan, between one and two, *e. g.* 'Not to outsport discretion,' II, 3, 3 ($\angle \smile \smile - \smile - \smile$).

This blending of dactyls with trochees produces a cadence that seemed to the Greeks to resemble the movement of their prose. Hence to such mixed staves they gave the name logaoedic, or prose-like.

Up to this point all the staves that have been shown have begun with an accented syllable. But in English poetry, from the beginning on, the habit has prevailed of setting, at the poet's convenience, before the first accent of the stave one unaccented syllable or even two. So Tennyson in the *Two Voices :*

> Again the voice spake unto me,
> 'Thou art so full of misery,
> Surely 'twere better not to be.'

Here in the same stanza, in rhyming lines of
the closest correspondence, the third stave
begins with an accented syllable, but the first
and the second begin with syllables that are
unaccented.

This unaccented syllable that goes before
the first accent of the stave bears the technical
name of anacrusis. It is the preparation, the
prelude to the stave, a mechanical means of
giving force to the following accent. The
presence of the anacrusis gives rise, therefore,
to certain additional forms of the English
stave.

The stave that has the anacrusis before a
trochee is called an iambic stave, *e. g.* 'And
prays you to believe him,' I, 3, 42 (× | ᷆ ᴗ ‒
ᴗ ‒ ᴗ).

The stave that has one anacrusis or two
before a dactyl is called anapaestic, *c. g.* 'O
villany, villany,' V, 2, 193 (× | ᷆ ᴗ ᴗ ‒ ᴗ ᴗ).

The stave that has the anacrusis before a
logaoedic measure may be called loose iambic,
e. g. 'To bear him easily hence,' V, 1, 83
(× | ᷆ ᴗ ‒ ᴗ ᴗ ‒).

Thus we reach a grouping of possible English staves that is adequate for our purposes. According to length, the staves of English poetry are staves of 1 accent, or of 2, or of 3 or 4, either catalectic or full. According to arrangement of accents, they are trochaic, or dactylic, or logaoedic, or iambic, or loose iambic. For convenience of classification, the staves of which English poetry is formed may be arranged into a table of 22 varieties.

Staves of one accent:

    1. Trochaic ∠◡.

    2. Dactylic ∠◡◡.

    3. Iambic × | ∠◡.

    4. Anapaestic × | ∠◡◡ or × × | ∠◡◡.

Staves of two accents:

    5. Trochaic ∠◡–◡ or ∠◡–.

    6. Dactylic ∠◡◡–◡◡ or ∠◡◡–.

    7. Logaoedic ∠◡◡–◡ or ∠◡–◡◡.

    8. Iambic × | ∠◡–◡ or × | ∠◡–.

    9. Anapaestic × | ∠◡◡–◡◡ or × × | ∠◡◡–◡◡.

    10. Loose iambic × | ∠◡–◡◡.

Staves of three accents:

11. Trochaic ´◡–◡–◡ with sub-forms.
12. Dactylic ´◡◡–◡◡–◡◡ "
13. Logaoedic ´◡◡–◡–◡ "
14. Iambic × | ´◡–◡–◡ "
15. Anapaestic × | ´◡◡–◡◡–◡◡ with sub-forms.
16. Loose iambic × | ´◡◡–◡–◡ with sub-forms.

Staves of four accents:

17. Trochaic ´◡–◡–◡–◡ with sub-forms.
18. Dactylic ´◡◡–◡◡–◡◡–◡◡ with sub-forms.
19. Logaoedic ´◡◡–◡–◡–◡ with sub-forms.
20. Iambic × | ´◡–◡–◡–◡ with sub-forms.
21. Anapaestic × | ´◡◡–◡◡–◡◡– with sub-forms.
22. Loose iambic × | ´◡◡–◡–◡–◡ with sub-forms.

These twenty-two staves are the material out of which Shakspere's verse is constructed. But, before we discuss his manner of using them, there is one other variation of stave-

form so important as to demand careful notice.

The full foot of English poetry is either a
trochee or a dactyl; it has after its accented
syllable either one or two unaccented. The
length of the entire foot is divided between
the time given to the strong syllable and the
time given to the weak syllable. Thus in the
trochaic foot *beggar*, the strong syllable *beg* is
rather more than twice as long as the weak
syllable *ar*. But now, to gain some special
purpose, to throw unusual force into some
emphatic word, the weak syllable of the foot
may be altogether suppressed, and the entire
length of the whole foot concentrated upon
the accented syllable. Thus in the wild cry of
Othello, ' Oh! oh! oh!' V, 2, 282, the word
oh is by itself, each time, a separate foot, with
all its length and its force concentrated into
one syllable that is almost doubly long. Such
a foot is said to be syncopated. By syncope,
as is clear, the twenty-two varieties of the
English stave may be greatly modified in form
and in effect. Shakspere, above all, was very

bold in using the syncope, and the staves that contain syncopated feet are often conspicuous for their splendid energy of rhythm.

These twenty-two staves were the material out of which, by selection and by combination, Shakspere and his fellow-poets built up their system of dramatic verse. The staves themselves, as may be proved, were as old as the oldest utterance of Saxon poetry in the epos of heathen times. They were natural to the tongue and familiar to the ears of Englishmen. Holding fast to these forms of the long established English staves, let us now trace in detail how Shakspere used them as the units of his art to build up all the varieties of his infinitely modulated verse.

The verses of Shakspere, as seen in his dramas, fall into three kinds. They are: 1. his imperfect verses; 2. his broken verses; 3. his perfect verses.

The imperfect verses of Shakspere are characteristic of his art. They occur, I think, in all his dramas, but they occur oftenest in his mature work, where his art was at its

boldest and its best. So far from being signs
of careless workmanship, they come in passages of the most elaborate construction, in
the full career of his grandest poetry. Notice,
for example, the words by which Iago drives
his lord to madness, III, 3, 413-18 :

> I will go on.   I lay with Cassio lately,
> And, being troubled with a raging tooth,
> *I could not sleep.*
> There are a kind of men so loose of soul
> That in their sleeps will mutter their affairs.
> *One of this kind is Cassio.*

Notice again the words of Othello, as, con-
vinced at last of his wife's innocence, he takes
his final look at her dead face, V, 2, 274-8 :

> This look of thine will hurl my soul from heaven,
> And fiends will snatch at it.   Cold, cold, my girl !
> Even like thy chastity.   O cursed slave !
> *Whip me, ye devils,*
> From the possession of this heavenly sight !

Such, then, are the imperfect verses of
Shakspere, often the most sonorous and
splendid of his rhythmical effects. In studying
them the value of Dr. Guest's system of staves
comes into the clearest evidence. For these

imperfect verses of Shakspere are nothing but the simple staves of the English language used in one or other of their twenty-two primitive forms. Each one of Shakspere's imperfect verses is in reality a simple stave seized by the genius of the poet and cast forth by him to live as a separate verse. In the Othello I find 263 imperfect verses out of the entire number of 2837 verses, or about one in eleven. They reduce themselves, including syncopated staves, to 31 varieties of construction.

I. Imperfect verses of trochaic type:

1. Monopody, occurring four times, *e. g.*
   'Devil!' IV, 1, 251.
2. Dipody, occurring seven times, *e. g.*
   'What's the matter?' IV, 1, 50.
3. Dipody catalectic, occurring six times,
   'Do thy worst,' V, 2, 159.
4. Tripody, occurring eight times, *e. g.*
   'Let her have your voices,' I, 3, 261.
5. Tripody catalectic, occurring once,
   'Are you sure of that?' IV, 1, 238.
6. Tetrapody, occurring twice, *e. g.*
   'You have little cause to say so,' II, 1, 109.

7. Tetrapody catalectic, occurring once,
   'Will you come to bed, my lord?' V,
   2, 24.

II. Imperfect verses of dactylic type:

8. Dipody catalectic, occurring sixteen times,
   'Show me thy thought,' III, 3, 116.

III. Imperfect verses of iambic type:

9. Monopody, occurring eleven times, *e. g.*
   'Abhor me,' I, 1, 6.

10. Monopody catalectic, occurring four-
teen times, *e. g.*
   'Indeed!' III, 3, 101.

11. Dipody, occurring twenty-one times,
   'And in conclusion,' I, 1, 15.

12. Dipody catalectic, occurring thirty-four
times, *e. g.*
   'And what was he?' I, 1, 18.

13. Tripody, occurring thirty times, *e. g.*
   'And prays you to believe him,' I, 3, 42.

14. Tripody catalectic, occurring forty-one
times, *e. g.*
   'As if the case were his,' III, 3, 4.

15. Tetrapody, occurring once,
   'A Florentine more kind and honest,'
      III, 1, 43.

16. Tetrapody catalectic, occurring twenty-one times, *e. g.*

> 'How now! what do you here alone?'
> III, 3, 300.

IV. Imperfect verses of logaoedic type:

17. Dipody, occurring five times, *e. g.*

> 'Say it, Othello,' I, 3, 127.

18. Tripody, occurring five times, *e. g.*

> 'One of this kind is Cassio,' III, 3, 418.

19. Tripody catalectic, occurring eleven times, *e. g.*

> 'What is the matter there?' I, 1, 83.

20. Tetrapody catalectic, occurring once,

> 'Nobody: I myself: farewell,' V, 2, 124.

V. Imperfect verses of anapaestic type:

21. Tripody catalectic, occurring three times,

> 'I might do't as well i' the dark,' IV, 3, 67.

22. Tetrapody catalectic, occurring seven times, but only in song, IV, 3, 43 *seq.*

23. Dipody, occurring once,

> 'O villany, villany!' V, 2, 193.

VI. Imperfect verses of loose iambic type:

24. Dipody, occurring once, in song, IV, 3, 42.

25. Tripody, occurring once,

'Is spied in populous cities,' I, 1, 77.

26. Tripody catalectic, occurring once, in song, II, 3, 75.

VII. Imperfect verses of syncopated type:

27. Syncope in first foot of dipody, occurring once, viz.

'Down, strumpet!' V, 2, 79.

28. Syncope in first foot of catalectic dipody, occurring five times, *e. g.*

'Thieves! thieves!' I, 1, 81.

29. Syncope in first and second foot of tripody, occurring twice, *e. g.*

'O blood, blood, blood!' III, 3, 451.

30. Syncope in first foot of tetrapody, occurring once,

'News, lads! our wars are done," II, 1, 20.

31. Syncope in third foot of tetrapody, a "halting rhythm," occurring once in song, II, 3, 99.

The broken verses of Shakspere form a
class that has been the despair of editors.
They have a strongly marked character, de-
fying utterly the rules of scansion by feet, and
seeming at first sight irregular and lawless.
For the most part such broken verses are
divided between two persons of the dialogue :
the first half belongs to one speaker, the
second half to another, *e. g.*

(Desdemona speaks.) Who's there? Othello?—
(Othello replies.) Ay, Desdemona. V, 2, 23.

a broken verse of four accents.

Gratiano. What is the matter?—*Othello.* Behold, I
have a weapon. V, 2, 259.

a broken verse of five accents.

Montano. For 'tis a damned slave.—*Othello.* I am not
valiant neither. V, 2, 243.

a broken verse of six accents.

Othello. She was false as water.—*Emilia.* Thou art
rash as fire to say. V, 2, 134.

a broken verse of seven accents.

In other cases the broken verse is not
broken by the change of the person speaking,
but by the change of the person addressed.

The speaker directs the first part of the verse to one character, the second part to another, *e. g.*

> O, that's an honest fellow.—Do not doubt Cassio.
>
> III, 3, 4.

where Othello speaks first to Emilia, and then by abrupt change to Cassio.

Still in other cases the broken verse is not broken by the change either of the speaker or of the person addressed. It is broken by some violent change of emotion; the first part is spoken in one mood, the second part in another.

Broken verses of the three kinds make up together a large element in Shakspere's dramatic poetry. In the Othello I count 252 broken verses, or about nine per cent of the entire number. And in making this count I have left out all forms of broken verses that are identical in construction with forms of perfect verses, to be considered hereafter. If we examine these 252 broken verses, we shall find them all to be incapable of scansion by feet. But here again, if we try the system of scansion by staves, all becomes at once regular. Each broken verse is found to consist of either two or three perfect staves; and all the apparent lawlessness disappears when each part of the verse is uttered as an independent stave. Just as the imperfect verses of Shakspere are one or other of the 22 stave-forms taken separately, so the broken verses are two or three of these same staves, each complete in itself, simply added together.

The varieties of staves that are used in forming the broken verses are generally the same as in the imperfect verses. The trochaic, the iambic, and the logaoedic staves are exactly the same, without new forms; cf. pp. 25 and 26. The dactylic staves, however, are more freely admitted. So the dactylic dipody is used in the first part of the difficult verse:

'Players in your housewifery, and housewives in your beds,' II, 1, 113,

and the dactylic tripody is used in the second part of

'O monstrous act!—Villany, villany, villany!'

The anapaestic dipody catalectic is found in the broken verse with its anacrusis of two syllables.   So in the first part of

> ' Not a jot, not a jot.—I' faith, I fear it
> has,' III, 3, 215.

This use of the double anacrusis we shall find later on among the perfect verses.

The number of forms that belong to the loose iambic class, cf. p. 28, is much larger among the broken than among the imperfect verses.

Dipody with dactyl in second place, *e. g.*

> ' For nought but provender —and when
> he's old cashiered,' I, 1, 48.

Tripody with dactyl in first place, *e. g.*

> ' Indeed, they are disproportioned,' I, 3, 2.

Tripody with dactyl in second place, *e. g.*

> 'What's the matter, lieutenant?' II, 3, 150.

Tripody with dactyl in third place, *e. g.*

> 'And sing it like poor Barbara,' IV, 3, 33.

The syncopated staves occur in many varieties among the broken verses.

The dipody, syncopated in first foot, occurs in the second half of IV, 2, 90:

> 'that married with Othello — You, mistress ';

and with anacrusis in the second half of V, 1, 100:

> 'I'll fetch the general's surgeon — For you, mistress.'

The tripody, syncopated in first foot, occurs in first half of I, 1, 119:

> 'This thou shalt answer—I know thee Roderigo.'

The tripody, syncopated in second foot, occurs in the second half of V, 1, 105:

> 'Stay you, good gentlemen.—Look you pale, mistress ?'

The tripody catalectic, syncopated in first foot, occurs in first part of II, 1, 25:

> 'How! is this true?—The ship is here put in ';

cf. I, 3, 400, II, 3, 158, II, 3, 168, III, 3, 176, III, 3, 393.

The tetrapody, syncopated in the first foot, occurs in second half of IV, 1, 61 :

> 'Dost thou mock me?—I mock you! no,
>   by heaven.'

The tetrapody catalectic, syncopated in the first foot, occurs in second half of I, 2, 53 :

> 'Marry to—Come, captain, will you go?'

cf. III, 4, 44.

In conclusion, if we add to the 31 stave-forms that occur in the imperfect verses the 13 stave-forms that occur only in the broken verses, we may assert 44 distinct stave-forms to exist in the Othello, as. the elements of Shakspere's verse.

We pass now to the third kind of verse used by Shakspere, the perfect verse. It has the regular five accents of the pentapody, and forms of course the great body of the rhythmical drama. Let us take as example:

> 'If thou dost slander her and torture me,
> Never pray more; abandon all remorse:
> On horror's head horrors accumulate.'
>
> > III, 3, 368-70.

All these verses are perfect verses, yet each is

different from the others, and the great movement goes on with an infinite variety of shifted
cadences.

V. 368 has its caesura after *her:* it breaks
into two parts, of six and four syllables
respectively.

V. 369 has its caesura after *more :* it breaks
into two parts, of four and six syllables respectively.

V. 370 has its caesura after *head:* it breaks
again into two parts, of four and six syllables
respectively. But here the variety of movement is won by letting the accented syllable
head come next to the accented syllable of
horrors, that is, by admitting the syncopated
foot.

Each verse is thus seen to be cloven in
twain by the pause that we call caesura ; each
verse consists of two parts divided by caesura.
Each of these parts may now be separately
examined.

'If thou dost slander her' is an iambic stave
of three accents.

'and torture me' is an iambic stave of two
accents.

' Nẹver pray mọre' is a dactylic stave of two accents.

' abạndon ạll remọrse' is an iambic stave of three accents.

' On họrror's heạd' is an iambic stave of two accents.

' họrrors accụmulạte' is a logaoedic stave of three accents.

The analysis of these three verses leads us to seize the law of Shakspere's verse-construction. The perfect verse of Shakspere is formed in every case by so jointing two separate staves to each other as to produce a full verse of five accents. In the broken verse the second stave is simply added to the first without any reciprocal adaptation. But in the perfect verse the beginning of the second stave is fitted on to the end of the first: the caesural pause is so managed as to let the voice glide from the one stave into the other. And, while the sum of the two staves may in the broken verse be four accents, or five, or six, or even seven, the sum of the two staves in the perfect verse is always five accents, a pentapody.

From the point now reached we can form an adequate conception both of the perfect regularity of Shakspere's art and of its vast possibilities of variation. To make his perfect verse one stave must be joined on to another so as to give the sum of five accents. Now of stave-forms there were, cf. pp. 20–21, twenty-two distinct types; and each of these twenty-two forms might occur either full or catalectic, and each might be varied by the use of syncopated feet. It needs but a grammarian's knowledge of arithmetic to show us that, by combining the staves, Shakspere had at his command many thousands, a practical infinity, of distinct verse-forms. Thus, in his art, the stave was the unit of all his combinations. Each stave, taken by itself, could form one of his imperfect verses. Two staves added together made one of his broken verses, a compound verse of four or five or six or seven accents. Finally, two staves so dove-tailed by caesura as to give an artistic unity of five accents made his perfect verse, the infinitely varied pentapody.

Among all these thousands of possible forms, the genius of the poet guided him to pick and select according to some mysterious sense of harmony. Some combinations were ugly and he did not use them at all. Others had capacity for a certain effect, and he used them when that effect was needed. Others still were easy and beautiful, and he used them over and over again with loving preference. To each phase of emotion certain forms of verse had in his mind a special adaptation. To each prominent character he gave as part of the individuality a certain predominant form of versification. Thus the verse-forms used by Othello are different from Iago's, and Desdemona's are again different from both the others'.[1] Our minds are hardly able to grasp

---

[1] It may be of interest to see in detail the characteristics of the verse-forms used by Desdemona, by Othello, and by Iago, and to note their differences. The basis of comparison is the number of perfect verses spoken by each in third and fourth acts, all imperfect and broken verses being omitted.

1. Let all verses be considered normal that contain only trochaic feet, and all abnormal that contain either dactylic or syncopated feet.

the immensity of the great poet's rhythmical resources. But in the poet himself,

---

Desdemona has 83 per cent of normal verses to 17 per cent of abnormal.

Othello has 59 per cent of normal verses to 41 per cent of abnormal.

Iago has 59 per cent of normal verses to 41 per cent of abnormal.

2. Let the verse of feminine ending be considered a full verse, and the verse of masculine ending a catalectic verse.

Desdemona has 77 per cent of catalectic verses to 23 per cent full.

Othello has 72 per cent of catalectic verses to 28 per cent full

Iago has 64 per cent of catalectic verses to 36 per cent full.

3. Let the comparison be made in respect of the use made by each of masculine and feminine caesuras.

Desdemona has 65 per cent of masculine caesuras to 35 per cent of feminine.

Othello has 63 per cent of masculine caesuras to 37 per cent of feminine.

Iago has 52 per cent of masculine caesuras to 48 per cent of feminine.

4. Let the comparison be made in respect of the admission of dactylic feet.

Desdemona has 20 dactylic feet in 100 verses.

Othello   "   42   "   "

Iago   "   51   "   "

5 Let the comparison be made in respect of the admission of syncopated feet.

as he ripened in age and in art, the habits
and preferences of his versification changed.

Desdemona has 3 syncopated feet in 100 verses.
Othello   " 11   "   "
Iago   " 10   "   "

6. Finally, let the comparison be made in respect of
the predominating types of verse-form used by each.

Desdemona has 34 per cent with masculine caesura
after 3d accent ; 27 per cent with masculine caesura
after 2d accent; 19 per cent with feminine caesura
after 2d trochee ; 9 per cent with feminine caesura
after 3d trochee.

Othello has 25 per cent with masculine caesura after
2d accent ; 24 per cent with masculine caesura after
3d accent; 16 per cent with feminine caesura after 2d
trochee ; 16 per cent with feminine caesura after 3d
trochee.

Iago has 27 per cent of masculine caesuras after 2d
accent; 27 per cent of feminine caesuras after 2d
trochee ; 16 per cent of feminine caesuras after 3d
trochee ; 13 per cent of masculine caesuras after 3d
accent.

The facts thus tabulated show, I think, a steady
correspondence and harmony between the character of
the person that speaks and the verse-forms that are
used. In Shakspere's art each verse-form has by its
predominance an ethical import. Thus, for example,
the verse-forms of Desdemona are dainty, regular and
equable. Of her verses 83 per cent are normal, only
17 abnormal. The even flow of her verses is disturbed
by only 20 dactyls in 100 lines, and by only 3 syncopes.
The endings of her verses are regular, or catalectic, 77

The range of his combinations became vaster;
the boldness of his touch, the variety of his

times in the 100, and full only 23 times. So too she
has a marked preference for the masculine caesura over
the feminine, giving 65 per cent of the one to 35 of
the other. In all these points the lovely verse-form of
Desdemona is distinguished by regularity, smoothness,
and the lack of all disturbing eccentricities: it is the
speech and manner of the high-bred, delicate lady.

As against this, the verse-forms of Othello and Iago
are marked by greater freedom and audacity of movement. Thus, while Desdemona had 83 normal verses
to 17 abnormal, Othello and Iago have only 59 normal
verses to 41 abnormal. While Desdemona had only
23 per cent of full verses, Othello had 28 per cent, and
Iago had 36 per cent. And again, while Desdemona
had only 20 dactylic feet in 100 lines, Othello had 42
and Iago 51. So too, while Desdemona used only 3
syncopated feet in 100 lines, Iago uses 10 and Othello
11. In all these things the verse-forms of Othello and
Iago show, as compared with Desdemona's, a bolder
license, a far greater sweep and rush of rhythmical
forms.

But the verse-forms of Othello and Iago, if compared
with each other, show again certain characteristic
differences Thus, while Othello has only 28 full
endings in 100 lines, Iago has 36. While Othello uses
42 dactyls in 100 lines, Iago uses 51. Above all, while
Othello keeps a large predominance of masculine
caesuras, 63 to 37, Iago has an almost exact equality
between them, 52 to 48. In all these things it may be
said that the verse-forms of Iago, as compared with

effects became greater. In Shakspere's verse, as in Burke's prose and in Turner's painting, the progress of art-growth was always toward freedom and audacity.

From the demonstration given above it would seem to follow that the right way of studying the verse of Shakspere is to study the arrangement and combination of the staves. The true metrical tests are to be found by comparing the use made by him, in his different styles and at his different times, of the simple staves out of which his verses are constructed. Were each play to be studied in this fashion, and the results tabulated, we should be able to follow the growth of his rhythmical art, and to construct the criteria for the age and the authorship of the plays. We could thus gain an exact knowledge of the types of verse used in each play, and could show for each play how many types occur, and how often each

---

Othello's, are rougher and harsher, not bolder indeed nor freer, but less sonorous and less beautiful. It is strange to see that the verse-form most largely used by Desdemona, the type with masculine caesura after third accent, is the one most rarely used by Iago.

type is used. Meanwhile it is possible, by the study of the Othello alone, a play of the poet's mature manner, to fix the leading types of Shakspere's verse, and to afford a basis of comparison for other plays.

In fixing the types of Shaksperian verse the chief points to be observed are these five: 1. The nature of the caesura, whether masculine or feminine; 2. The place of the caesura; 3. The nature of the ending, whether full (feminine) or catalectic (masculine); 4. The admission of the dactylic foot; 5. The admission of the syncopated foot.

The nature of caesura, whether masculine or feminine, has a very strong effect upon the movement and character of the verse. In the Othello the masculine predominates over the feminine in the general proportion of six to four. The exact numbers are given in the following table, in which count has been made of the 1634 normal verses that the play contains.

The 1st act contains 214 masculine caesuras and 171 feminine; 2d act, 163 masculine

caesuras and 113 feminine; 3d act, 249 masculine caesuras and 173 feminine; 4th act, 168
masculine caesuras and 89 feminine; 5th act,
184 masculine caesuras and 110 feminine.

The proportion is not absolutely uniform.
Among the normal verses of the entire poem
60 per cent have masculine caesura; but in
the 1st act the proportion is 56 to 44, in the
2d act 59 to 41, in the 3d act 59 to 41, in the
4th act 65 to 35, and in the 5th act 63 to 37.
The variation is not very large, and it stands
connected in some mysterious way with the
character of the speaking persons. In Iago's
speech, as we have seen, the feminine caesura
predominates over the masculine.

Again, the place of the caesura, whether
near the middle of the verse, or near the
beginning or the end, has a very strong effect
upon the movement of the rhythm. Placed
near the middle, it gives to the verse a regular
and even movement; placed near the beginning or near the end, it gives a movement that
is irregular and violent. Among the normal
verses of the Othello, 1634 in number, the

eight forms of possible caesura occur in the
following proportion in the five acts :

Masculine caesura after first accent, $6 + 3$
$+ 9 + 5 + 1 = 24$ in 5 acts.

Feminine caesura after 1st trochee, $19 + 9$
$+ 10 + 12 + 12 = 62$ in 5 acts.

Masculine caesura after 2d accent, $113 + 85$
$+ 117 + 80 + 98 = 493$ in 5 acts.

Feminine caesura after 2d trochee, $88 + 63$
$+ 104 + 35 + 66 = 356$ in 5 acts.

Masculine caesura after 3d accent, $87 + 70$
$+ 119 + 80 + 81 = 437$ in 5 acts.

Feminine caesura after 3d trochee, $64 + 41$
$+ 59 + 42 + 32 = 238$ in 5 acts.

Masculine caesura after 4th accent, $8 + 5$
$+ 4 + 3 + 4 = 24$ in 5 acts.

Feminine caesura after 4th trochee, 0.

The distribution is, throughout the five acts,
about the same ; the workmanship of Shakspere is equable and uniform. The caesuras
cluster thick about the middle of the verse, and
are rare near beginning and near end. In
other words, the staves that are best liked are
dipodies and tripodies.

In the next place, the ending of the verse,
whether full or catalectic, that is, whether weak
or strong, is another important criterion in
fixing the types of Shaksperian verse. The
verse that ends with a full trochee ends with a
falling cadence; the verse that ends with a
catalectic trochee ends with a rising cadence.
Each has its peculiar and calculable effect, *e. g.*

> ' I see, sir, you are eaten up with passion :
> I do repent me that I put it to you.' III, 3, 391-2.

a couplet in which both verses are full, with
weak ending; and

> ' O monstrous world ! take note, take note, O world !
> To be direct and honest is not safe.'   III, 3, 377-8.

a couplet in which both verses are catalectic,
with strong ending.

To this point, however, great attention has
been given by one school of Shaksperian
scholars, and little remains to do. In the
Othello, taken altogether, the proportion of
full verses to catalectic is 27 to 73. The distribution of the full verses is right equable,
30 per cent in the 1st act, 24 per cent in

the 2d, 28 per cent in the 3d, 28 per cent in
the 4th, and 24 per cent in the 5th. In dealing
with these full verses one habit of Shakspere
is worth noting. The peculiar swing of their
movement is best felt when they are massed
together in rhythmical groups. Thus a great
proportion of his full verses is found in
sequences of two, three, four, five, or even six
verses, *e. g.* I, 3, 111–116 :

Senator.
Did you by indirect and forced courses
Subdue and poison this young maid's affections?
Or came it by request and such fair question
As soul to soul affordeth ?
Othello. I do beseech you,
Send for the lady to the Sagittary,
And let her speak of me before her father.

The fourth point to watch, in fixing the type
of Shakspere's verses, is the admission of the
dactyl. The absence of dactyls, as we saw in
Desdemona's speech, is the mark of regular
and equable movement; the frequency of
dactyls is the measure of excitement and dis-
turbance. Thus, among the broken verses,
dactylic feet are far more numerous than

among the perfect verses. Of 252 broken verses, 108 have dactyls in one or more feet, about 42 per cent. The distribution of dactylic verses among the successive acts is tolerably uniform: 15 per cent in the 1st act, 20 per cent in the 2d, 23 per cent in the 3d, 17 per cent in the 4th, and 19 per cent in the 5th. But the proportion varies both according to the nature of the scene and according to the character of the person speaking. The speech of Iago, for example, is marked by a strong predominance of dactyls, that of Desdemona by rarity of dactyls. Here too, as in the case of the full endings, the poet loves to bring out the force of the dactylic feet by massing them into groups of successive verses, *e. g.* I, 1, 149–155. The favorite place for the dactyl is the 1st foot of the first stave, where it occurs 251 times; in the 2d foot it occurs 76 times, in the 3d foot 52 times, in the 4th foot 41 times, in the 5th foot only twice.' In addition there are 42 verses that have two dactyls each, and one verse that has three dactyls.

---

¹ In this count the broken verses are not included, only the perfect verses.

The last point to be noted, in fixing the types of Shakspere's verses, is the admission of syncopated feet. Among the 252 broken verses I find 13 cases of syncope. Among the perfect verses I find 78 cases of syncope : 14 in the 1st act, 10 in the 2d, 20 in the 3d, 13 in the 4th, and 21 in the 5th. The percentage is too small to make any calculation valuable. In respect of the place preferred, the syncope differs strangely from the dactyl. Dactyls are greatly more numerous at the beginning of the pentapody, and diminish in number by regular gradation to the end. Syncopes are greatly more numerous at the middle of the verse, and are equally rare at the beginning and the end. Among the perfect verses of the five acts, the 3d foot of the pentapody is syncopated 39 times ; the 2d, 25 times ; the 1st, 7 times ; the 4th, 7 times.

It remains then, in order to bring this essay to its end, to give a classified list of those types of perfect verse that exist in the Othello. It will be convenient to give first the normal types, which contain neither dactylic nor syncopated feet, and then the abnormal types, which contain either the one or the other or both.

A. Normal types of verse.

I. Full verse, with masculine caesura after first accent ; *e. g.*

' Her will, ‖ recoiling to her better judgment,' or × | ´‖◡´◡´◡—◡—◡—◡.　　　III, 3, 236.

II. Catalectic verse with masculine caesura after first accent, *e. g.*

Exist, ‖ and be a member of his love
Whom I, ‖ with all the office of my heart.
or, × | ´‖◡´◡´◡—◡—◡—.　　　III, 4, 111–12.

Of types I and II, taken together, with masculine caesura after first accent, I find 28 examples in the play : 6 in the 1st act, 3 in the 2d, 9 in the 3d, 5 in the 4th, and 5 in the 5th. The type is rare.

III. Full verse with masculine caesura after fourth accent, *e. g.*

I had rather to adopt a child.‖ than get it.
　　　　　　　　　　　　　I, 3, 191.

(I had = I'd as one syllable in anacrusis),
or × | ⏑⏑–⏑–⏑–‖⏑⏑⏑.

IV. Catalectic verse with masculine caesura
after fourth accent, *e. g.*

Nor scar that whiter skin of hers ‖ than snow.
or × | ⏑⏑–⏑–⏑–‖⏑⏑.   V, 2, 4.

Of types III and IV, taken together, with
masculine caesura after fourth accent, I find
24 examples in the play: 8 in the 1st act, 5 in
the 2d, 4 in the 3d, 3 in the 4th, and 4 in the
5th. The type is rare.

V. Full verse with masculine caesura after
second accent, *e. g.*

I'll watch him tame ‖ and talk him out of
  patience.   III, 3, 23.
or × | ⏑⏑–‖⏑⏑⏑–⏑–⏑.

VI. Catalectic verse with masculine caesura
after second accent, *e. g.*

And, on the proof, ‖ there is no more but this:
Away at once ‖ with love or jealousy!
or × | ⏑⏑–‖⏑⏑⏑–⏑–.   III, 3, 191–2.

Of types V and VI, taken together, with masculine caesura after second accent, I find 495 examples in the play: 114 in the 1st act, 85 in the 2d, 119 in the 3d, 80 in the 4th, and 97 in the 5th. The type is much beloved by Shakspere, and its peculiar equable movement is felt in passages where the form is maintained throughout many consecutive verses, *e. g.* IV, 3, 97–102, with exception of 98.

VII. Full verse with masculine caesura after third accent, *e. g.*

Whatever shall become || of Michael Cassio,
He's never any thing || but your true servant.
or × | ́∪–∪–||́∪–∪.   III, 3, 8–9.

VIII. Catalectic verse with masculine caesura after third accent, *e. g.*

Why, then, to-morrow night || or Tuesday
   morn :
On Tuesday noon or night: || on Wednesday
   morn :
I prithee, name the time, || but let it not . . .
or × | ́∪–∪–||∪ ́∪–.   III, 3, 60–62.

Of types VII and VIII, taken together, with masculine caesura after third accent, I find in the play 438 examples: 87 in the 1st act, 70 in the 2d, 119 in the 3d, 80 in the 4th, and 82 in the 5th. This again, then, is a form much beloved by Shakspere; and he likes to bring out its peculiar movement by long series of consecutive verses, *e. g.* Othello's speech, II, 3, 207–212.

IX. Full verse with feminine caesura after first trochee, *e. g.*

I see, sir, ‖ you are eaten up with passion.
or x | ´◡‖´◡–◡–◡–◡.   III, 3, 391.

X. Catalectic verse with feminine caesura after first trochee, *e. g.*

Come, mistress, ‖ you must tell's another tale,
Emilia, ‖ run you to the citadel.
or x | ´◡‖´◡–◡–◡–.   V, 1, 125–6.

Of types IX and X, taken together, with feminine caesura after first trochee, I find in the play 62 examples: 19 in the 1st act, 9 in the 2d, 10 in 3d, 12 in 4th, and 12 in 5th. The type is rare.

XI. Full verse with feminine caesura after second trochee, *e. g.*

You, Rọderigo ! ‖ cọme, sir, I am fọr you.
Keep up your bright swords ; fọr the dẹw will
    rụst them.   I, 2, 58–9.
or x | ∠∪–∪‖∠∪–∪–∪.

XII. Catalectic verse with feminine caesura after second trochee, *e. g.*

We lạcked your cọunsel ‖ ạnd your hẹlp to-
    night.   I, 3, 51.
or x | ∠∪–∪‖∠∪–∪–.

Of types XI and XII, taken together, with feminine caesura after second trochee, I find in the play 358 examples: 89 in the 1st act, 63 in the 2d, 104 in the 3d, 36 in the 4th, and 66 in the 5th. For the sustained effect of this caesura see Emilia's speech, III, 3, 292–7.

XIII. Full verse with feminine caesura after third trochee, *e. g.*

Prefẹrment gọes by lẹtter ‖ ạnd affẹction
And nọt by ọld gradạtion, ‖ whẹre each sẹcond.
or x | ∠∪–∪–∪‖∠∪–∪.   I, 1, 36–7.

XIV. Catalectic verse with feminine caesura after third trochee, *e. g.*

I prattle out of fashion, ‖ and I dote.

or × | ∠∪–∪–∪‖∠∪–.   II, 1, 208.

Of types XIII and XIV, taken together, with feminine caesura after third trochee, I find in the play 238 examples: 64 in the 1st act, 41 in the 2d, 59 in the 3d, 42 in the 4th, and 32 in the 5th. Shakspere likes, it may be said, to combine this form of caesura with the full ending of the verse, *e. g.* Cassio's speech, II, 1, 97, 98, 99.

XV. Trochaic type, five trochees without anacrusis, *e. g.*

Full:

O most lame ‖ and impotent conclusion!

or ∠∪–‖∪ ∠∪–∪–∪.   II, 1, 161.

Do you triumph, Roman? ‖ Do you triumph?

or ∠∪–∪–∪‖∠∪–∪.   IV, 1, 121.

Catalectic:

Nor I neither ‖ by this heavenly light.

IV, 3, 66.

Ạy, with Cạssio. ‖ Nạy, had shẹ been trụe.
or ⌒∪–∪‖⌒∪–∪–. V, 2, 143.

The existence of this trochaic type has been
by some critics and grammarians denied.
Thus, for example, even in the Globe edition,
II, 1, 161, in spite of its markedly rhythmical character, is printed as prose. But
this verse-form, which makes a necessary link
in the development of English poetry, is in
itself altogether regular and agreeable; it was
beloved by Chaucer; it was used by Marlowe;
and thus it came of due right into the system
of Shakspere, *e. g.*

Cọnquer, sạck ‖ and ụtterly consụme.
Marlowe. Tamburlaine, Second Part, IV, 2.

Tẹar for tẹar, ‖ and lọving kịss for kịss.
Tit. Andr. V, 3, 156.

Such verses as these are too splendid in
rhythm to be given up in favor of any narrow
theory of iambic versification; and they teach
us, what so many other facts confirm, that the
presence or absence of the anacrusis is a
matter of indifference.

XVI. Verses of double anacrusis. Here the first trochee is preceded by two unaccented syllables, which can be pronounced together with great rapidity and ease, *e. g.*

Either in discourse of thought || or actual deed.

×× | ⌣⌣–⌣–||⌣⌣⌣–.   IV, 2, 153.

Cf. I, 3, 277, and *whether* in I, 1, 39, *he has*, I, 3, 394, etc., etc.

B. Abnormal types of verse.

XVII. Verses syncopated in the first foot. Full verse:

Here's one comes in his shirt, || with light and
  weapons.   V, 1, 47.

× | ⌣–⌣⌣–||⌣⌣⌣–⌣.

Catalectic verses:
  With one || of an ingraft infirmity.

× | ⌣||–⌣⌣⌣⌣–⌣–.   II, 3, 145.

To beguile many || and be beguiled by one.

×× | ⌣⌣⌣||⌣⌣⌣–⌣–.   IV, 1, 98.

As seen in this example, verses that are syncopated in the first foot are apt to begin with double anacrusis.

Of verses with first foot syncopated I find
3 in the 1st act, 2 in the 2d, 1 in the 3d, 1 in
the 4th, and one in the 5th, or only 8 in all.

XVIII. Verses syncopated in the second
foot.

Full verse :
Poor Cassio's smiles, || gestures and light be-
  haviour.   IV, 1, 103.
x | ⏑⏑∠ || ∠⏑⏑−⏑−⏑.

Catalectic verses :
  On horror's head || horror's accumulate.
x | ⏑⏑∠ || ∠⏑⏑−⏑−.   III, 3, 370.

Of verses with second foot syncopated I
find 3 in the 1st act, 3 in the 2d, 10 in the 3d,
3 in the 4th, and 3 in the 5th, 22 in all.

XIX. Verses syncopated in the third foot.

Full verse :
  My life upon her faith ! || Honest Iago.
x | ∠⏑−⏑∠ || ∠⏑⏑−⏑.   I, 3, 295.

Catalectic verse :
  'Tis not a year or two || shews us a man.
x | ∠⏑−⏑∠ || ∠⏑⏑−.   III, 4, 103.

Of verses with third foot syncopated I find 5 in the 1st act, 4 in the 2d, 8 in the 3d, 8 in the 4th, and 12 in the 5th, 37 in all.

XX. Verses syncopated in the fourth foot.

All such verses that I have found are catalectic. To syncopate the fourth foot and leave the fifth foot full would create the comical limping verse; and this Shakspere seems carefully to avoid.

Patience awhile, good Cassio.   Come, come!

´∪∪–∪–∪‖∠–.   V, 1, 87.

Farewell the neighing steed, and the shrill trump.   III, 3, 351.

× | ´∪–∪–‖∪∪∠–.

Of verses with fourth foot syncopated I find 3 in the 1st act, 1 in the 2d, 1 in the 3d, 1 in the 4th, and 1 in the 5th, only 7 in all.

XXI. Verses syncopated in two feet.

Syncopated in 2d and 3d feet:

The noise was here.   Ha! no more moving?

× | –∪∠‖∠´∪–∪.   V, 2, 93.

Other examples that might seem to belong to this type may be better explained as broken verses, made of two independent staves, *e. g.* V, 2, 337.

Of the syncopated types in general it may be said that syncope is more pleasing in the middle of verses and less pleasing at the beginning and end. Shakspere syncopates the third foot 38 times, the second foot 23 times, the first foot 8 times, and the fourth foot only 7 times.

XXII. Verses with dactyl in first foot preceded by anacrusis.

Full verse :
My daughter is not for thee: || and now in madness.   I, 1, 98.
x | ‒∪∪‒∪‒||∪‒∪‒∪.

Catalectic verse:
I'd whistle her off, || and let her down the wind.   III, 3, 262.
x | ‒∪∪‒||∪‒∪‒∪‒.

Of this type I find 8 verses in the 1st act, 3 in the 3d, 1 in the 4th, and 2 in the 5th, 14 in all.

XXIII. Verses without anacrusis, beginning
with dactyl in first foot. Lines of this majestic
rhythm form a large proportion of the verses
of Othello, and, coming often in groups of two
or three, give a special character to certain
grand passages.

Full verses:
Cassio, my lord! || No, sure, I cannot think it.

III, 3, 38.
Catalectic verses:
Poor and content is rich, || and rich enough.

III, 3, 172.

Of this type I find 39 verses in the 1st act,
58 in the 2d, 65 in the 3d, 30 in the 4th, and
47 in the 5th, 239 in all.

XXIV. Verses with dactyl in second foot.

Full verses:
And, lo, the happiness! || go and importune
her.   III, 4, 108.

× | ∠◡–◡◡||∠◡–◡–◡.

Catalectic verses:
O Desdemona! || away! away! away!

× | ∠◡–◡||◡∠◡–◡–.   IV, 2, 41.

The type is varied by the omission of anacrusis:

Made demonstrable here in Cyprus to him.

∠∪–∪∪‖∠∪–∪–∪.   III, 4, 142.

Of this type I find 14 verses in the 1st act,
9 in the 2d, 28 in the 3d, 12 in the 4th, and 15
in the 5th, 78 in all.

XXV. Verses with dactyl in 3d foot.

Full verse:

I am hitherto your daughter: ‖ but here's my
   husband.   I, 3, 185.

x | ∠∪–∪–∪‖∪∠∪–∪.

Catalectic verse:

Awake the snorting citizens ‖ with the bell.

                                 I, 1, 90.

x | ∠∪–∪–∪∪‖∠∪–.

As seen above, the dactyl in the third foot
is often preceded by syncope in the second, *e. g.*

On horror's head ‖ horrors accumulate.

                                 III, 3, 370.

Of this type I find 11 in the 1st act, 7 in
the 2d, 22 in the 3d, 6 in the 4th, and 6 in the
5th, 52 in all.

XXVI. Verses with dactyl in fourth foot.

Full verse :

There's many a beast then ‖ in a populous city.

× | -∪-∪‖∠∪ ∠∪∪-∪. IV, 1, 64.

Catalectic verse :

Of being taken ‖ by the insolent foe.

× | ∠∪-∪‖∠∪-∪∪-. I, 3, 137.

In many verses the dactyl of the fourth foot
is preceded and balanced by the syncope of the
third, *e. g.*

Hark, how these instruments ‖ summon to sup-
per ! IV, 2, 169.

× | ∠∪-∪∠‖∠∪∪-∪.

Of this type I find 3 in the 1st act, 6 in the
2d, 9 in the 3d, 9 in the 4th, and 13 in the 5th,
40 in all.

XXVII. Verses with dactyl in fifth foot.
The safe recognition of such verses is made
difficult by questions of pronunciation. Some
words, doubtless, standing thus at the end of
a verse, although they seem to us trisyllabic,
were in utterance dissyllables. These two

verses at least, however, seem unmistakable
examples of the type :

But he, ‖ as loving his own pride and purposes.   I, 1, 12.
× | ∠‖◡ ∠◡–◡–◡ ∠◡◡.

⸂Do you perceive ‖ in all this noble company.
× | ∠◡–‖◡ ∠◡–◡ ∠◡◡.   I, 3, 179.

XXVIII. Verses with dactyls both in first
and in second foot.

Full verses :
And yet he hath given me ‖ satisfying reasons.
× | ∠◡◡–◡◡‖∠◡–◡–◡.   V, 1, 9.

Catalectic verses :
Steeped me in poverty ‖ to the very lips.
× | –◡◡–◡◡‖∠◡–◡–.   IV, 2, 50.

Of this type I find 3 examples in the 1st
act, 5 in the 3d, 3 in the 4th, and 2 in the 5th,
13 in all.

XXIX. Verses with dactyls both in the first
foot and in the third.

Full verse :

This fortification, gentlemen, ‖ shall we see it?

x | ⌣⌣◡_◡_◡◡‖⌣◡_◡.   III, 2, 5.

Catalectic :

Naked in bed, Iago, ‖ and not mean harm !

⌣◡◡_◡⌣◡‖◡⌣◡_.   IV, 1, 5.

Of this type I find two examples in the 1st
act, 1 in the 2d, 5 in the 3d, 3 in the 4th, and
2 in the 5th, 13 in all.

XXX. Verses with dactyls both in the first
foot and in the fourth.

Full verses :

Blow me about in winds! ‖ roast me in sul-
   phur !   V, 2, 279.

⌣◡◡_◡◡⌞‖⌣◡◡_◡.

What is the reason ‖ of this terrible summons?

⌣◡◡_◡‖⌣◡_◡◡_◡.   I, 1, 82.

Catalectic verses :

Here is my journey's end, ‖ here is my butt.

⌣◡◡_◡⌞‖⌣◡◡_.   V, 2, 267.

Of this type I find 2 examples in the 1st
act, 1 in the 2d, and 4 in the 5th, 7 in all.

XXXI. Verse with dactyls both in the first foot and in the fifth.

(I do attach thee)
For an abaser of the world, ‖ a practiser.
∠ ∪ ∪ – ∪ – ∪ ∠ | ∪ ∠ ∪ ∪.   I, 2, 78.

Of this type I have not found another example in the Othello.

XXXII. Verses with dactyls both in the second foot and in the third. The full form of this type does not occur in the Othello.

Catalectic verses :
Or feed on nourishing dishes, ‖ or keep you
    warm.   III, 3, 78.
x | ∠ ∪ – ∪ ∪ – ∪‖∪ ∠ ∪ –.

Of hair-breadth scapes ‖ i' the imminent deadly
    breach.   I, 3, 136.
x | ∠ ∪ –‖∪ ∪ ∠ ∪ ∪ – ∪ –.

Two other examples occur (I, 1, 53 and I, 3, 49), four in all.

XXXIII. Verse with dactyls both in the second foot and in the fourth.

Full verse:

Set on thy wife to observe : leave me, Iago.

x | ᷄∪–∪ ∪ᷝ‖᷄∪∪–∪.   III, 3, 240.

Of this type I have not found another example.

XXXIV. Verses with dactyls both in the third foot and in the fourth. The full form of this type does not occur in the Othello.

Catalectic verses :

I had thought to have yerked him here ‖ under
the ribs.   II, 1, 15.

x | ᷄∪–∪–∪ ∪‖᷄∪∪–.

Two other examples occur (III, 3, 360 and III, 4, 80), three in all.

XXXV. Verses with three (3) dactyls.

Given to captivity ‖ me and my utmost hopes.
᷄∪∪–∪ ∪‖᷄∪∪–∪–.   IV, 2, 51.

This magnificent verse, standing alone in the Othello, seems to mark Shakspere's farthest range in the use of dactylic movements.

In the Othello, therefore, to sum up and tabulate the results as to Shakspere's use of the various types of perfect verse that he employed:

Verses, full or catalectic, with masculine caesura after 2d accent occur 495 times.

Verses, full or catalectic, with masculine caesura after 3d accent occur 438 times.

Verses, full or catalectic, with feminine caesura after 2d trochee occur 358 times.

Verses, with dactyl in 1st foot, without anacrusis occur 239 times.

Verses, full and catalectic, with feminine caesura after 3d trochee occur 238 times.

Verses dactylic in 2d foot occur 78 times.

Verses, full or catalectic, with feminine caesura after 1st trochee occur 62 times.

Verses dactylic in 3d foot occur 52 times.

Verses dactylic in 4th foot occur 40 times.

Verses syncopated in 3d foot occur 37 times.

Verses, full or catalectic, with masculine caesura after 1st accent occur 28 times.

Verses, full or catalectic, with masculine caesura after 4th accent occur 24 times.

Verses syncopated in 2d foot occur 22 times.

Verses dactylic in 1st foot, but preceded by anacrusis, occur 14 times.

Verses dactylic in 1st and 2d feet occur 13 times.

Verses dactylic in 1st and 3d feet occur 13 times.

Verses syncopated in 1st foot occur 8 times.

Verses syncopated in 4th foot occur 7 times.

Verses dactylic in 1st and 4th feet occur 7 times.

Verses dactylic in 2d and 3d feet occur 4 times.

Verses dactylic in 3d and 4th feet occur 3 times.

Verses entirely trochaic occur 3 times.

Verses dactylic in 5th foot occur twice.

Verse syncopated in 2 feet (2d and 3d) occurs once.

Verse dactylic in 1st and 5th feet occurs once.

Verse dactylic in 2d and 4th feet occurs once.

Verse dactylic in 1st, 2d, and 3d feet occurs once.

www.ingramcontent.com/pod-product-compliance
Lightning Source LLC
Chambersburg PA
CBHW031244260626
47169CB00007B/2446